WRECKING OF FRATERNITY

THE PETRIFY BLOODSHED

SUMEET KUMAR

ISBN 979-888546425-3

Sumeet Kumar

Sumeet Kumar , A adult who experiences many phases of love in his life , get broked many times , stands up every time and keep moving to the next phases of the life.In reality he is a writter as well as singer (as a hobby).

Very exciting and interesting fact about him is that he is aauthor of New era i.e. he starts his journey of writing at the age when he was going to schools to get the study . His some famous works i.e. Maturity Of Love (Genre - Love),Privacy For Dream (Genre - Middle Class), Army Squad ofLove (Genre- The Seperation of Army Love), 5 Days of Love(Genre- Temporarily Love), Th e Endearment Of Love(Genre - Historical Era Of Love), Social Destruction Indo-Pak (Genre - The Story of The Love At The Time Of Division Of India And Pakistan), Middle Class Soul (Genre - The Dreams of Middle Class), The Accursed Kanatpur (Genre -The Horrific Story Of A Village), Wrong Number (Genre -The Suspenseful Physco Killer Story), The Secrecy OfDeadly Midnight (Genre - The Suspense About a Crime),Fragile Religious Of Death (Genre- The Death Of A TrustfulPerson), Nature Vs Science (Genre - The Future Battle Between Nature And Science In A Horrific Way), Generic Man (Genre - The Dream of I.I.T), The Unconsious 12 Hours(Genre - The Illusion At Stage Of Comma), The StrangeBurden (Genre - The Burden Of Love) , Her Existence (Genre- The Female Pain In The Society) , Jockstrap Prize (Genre -The True Story Of A National Athlete) , H Man [Hindi] (Genre - Superhero Tragic Story), H Man [English] (Genre - Superhero Tragic Story) , Maturity Of Love [Englsih] (Genre - Love) and many more are available on various geners on the offcial platform of Amazon, Flipkart and Notionpress. You can buy them from there.

Contents

Preface

Love does not mean that it is always two sided, sometimes love is also one sided, which has no reason, if someone is in love: a moor comes where he is only and everywhere he looks deserted, then it is better that he has come to stay at the destination. Wasn't there in your part, it's better to go back to the destination where our silence is waiting. Sometimes it becomes a means. It is the means of love. If you will reveal it, then the right person only allows the pain to remain, which later on goes to someplace or other. If there was no age of love, then this person would have been dependent on God. There is no society in love. No caste because he himself has never been in love. It is the brothers and sisters who do not know today's society.

There is only hate everywhere, hate is uncountable, I don't say anything, I say enough, I say that remember the day when there was nothing other than our brotherhood, except love. Learn to love, talk and love, why not try to kishore religion .

Acknowledgements

Sumeet Kumar

Special Thanks to **Aman Kumar** who worked so hard in the preparation of this book. He has continually put with my passive voice, omission of words, and late night calls. You have be en wonderful. Thanks to him for his precious time in reviewing proposals , individual chapters

and early drafts, along with his suggestions on the
applicability of the material to the world.

• X •

CHAPTER ONE

Society Downfall

It is said that love is a means, it is a feeling that someone tells you to take it, be it a person, it may be his friends, even if it is to get out of the curse of something, even if the path sometimes comes in our stay, then it will give him the right foot only for a while. Never let the people come near, even if the mood changes, the feeling changes, the thinking of someone changes, the pond which is there to get someone, it also goes ahead and changes, the feet never love, because love is such an infatuation. The one who never stops for those who cry, say this, it is thirsty who has a lot of skill to say to someone. Why should his story remain incomplete? In today's age, there are very few people who have got their true love. They hand over the witnesses, with whom they are infatuated with love. It is not even strong that the thinking of this science has taken birth, it is its nib foot, our world is maintained, this our whole world has happened because of the shape of science , not at all because neither it has ever run from its principles, nor will it ever go, even if the line of thinking Science is in the hands of the feet, its handwriting is always of love, the creation of a house is not only because of it, nor even that too many times because of its root, from which it exists, it will not be able to take care of it going forward if it does not have love. Because in it The mixture of love is only such a moment, whose wish also gives you the unique life of the destiny of your existence. Let us become the means of every conversation and even when the whole world is against us, his love is his shadow and the writing of our fate, which has been created by the human God in the existence of human beings in our world, should continue to go ahead. Do it because true love She comes in the part of those who are unknown to each other. These days, where love is a deceit,love is a way to get one's own existence in their roti. Aqeeda, any enmity can destroy the existence of the world where science is protected, only love is fated. The more important thing than this is that the society does not accept that love should remain in their destiny because if we look back at the achievements of history. won the war enmity is only and only of male society, who have made all love as the means of the path. If I have any luck in my love then Oh, it is only this society and no one else because their baseless principles become the reason for all the time between some two lovers, even their feet are not aware of their own animosity, because today it is only arrogance who is trying to eradicate everything. Going forward, their existence will be left as the only blessing and nothing else. Veins that is till today you have used your sisters to live with each other.

Shayari 1

"TERI YAADEION KESAHARE HEEHAMSE AAJTAKMARG NE KOI RABTNA RAKHA.........KYUNKI JAB BHIUSKI AAHATMERE JUBAANPER AATI HAI....TERI YAADEION HEEUSH WAQTUSHE MITANEKI RIWAYATBANN JATI HAI .....MUQAABIL HUN TERAFURQAT KI WAJAHNA BANAAGAR RIWAYATKARNI HEE HAIMUJHE MITANE KITOH JARA USKIFAROGH TOH DIKHA ...."

CHAPTER TWO

War and Love

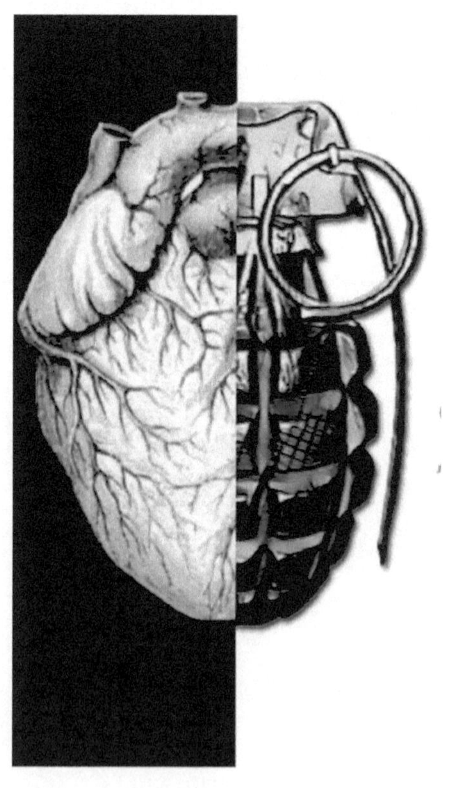

1920 Lahore This is not someone's story but it is a history of two lovers whose love for each other never changed. This story is of the same streets and localities where even though the pain butchery's feet are the happiness of the children, every day a new morning comes, even if the politics, the moving feet of the British, that kashryar was the only one whom we now know by the name of love, it is called love. There is a shadow from which humanity is never away from palaces. This story of a Romeo and Juliet is about those two lovers who have gone beyond these to get their love, whose names also match the tales of God. So let's know their love story and their love for such women Changed the handwriting of the line..and one more thing, even if the disciple I am pronunciation, but he will express his love himself. So this story is of a time when our country was not partitioned, I mean our mother India was not divided into two, our friendship was not broken into two, our love which was not divided between each other. There was a good time for them, they were not broken into two pieces, the journey is of happy destination, which was not made by God ever. K. Lee was fighting with the British, but in 1920, a boy was born in the house of a landowner, whose name was interpretation. He used to love and respect him, why did he face any problem in the village, he used to take people of his surgery problems to him, he was the only person of that village whose fate was not written in the hands of the British, even if he would give marriage. At the behest of the king of the British, he did not at all. By the way, Tabir's father His name was Dushyant Chowdarya, who belonged to a family whose genetics were never slaves of anyone. I didn't mean that we are slaves to only one thing in this world, he is only the love of that God and nothing else because neither we are his slaves. We are not afraid of writing, nor is the passion given to us by fate. They also wished that if you are unaware of something, then the only way for it to be born is called love, because love is the reason why you become a opponent of another. If there was no love for separation, then the destination on which we are walking would have been our own way. Till their love was not made for them. Because their love which they have for our country, they never worked in death, they never gave birth to God, nor ever thought of anything else in the eyes of their love for their country, because even at the same time their pond It was their love that was alive till date in our country in the year 1920, where interpretation was born, because of the Muslims. Aqeeda also took birth in the war, it is said that those who have love, the writing of their lines is also similar to each other, by the way, let me also tell that the family to which Aqeeda belonged was not a big family, I mean neither he There was a big landowner like Dushyant Chaudarya, according to business, Abu Jan was a blacksmith. It is not found that Tabeer's family and Aqeeda's family belonged to two different religions, even though their father was a very good friend, from childhood, both of them taught together since childhood that I should play with myself. I used to go to school and many more on the day Aqeeda and Tabeer were born, it was decided that Aqeeda Chaudrya family would become a daughter-in-law and no one else, by the way, forget to mention that Aqeeda's father's name was Safar Khan, who was a very good person. And whenever Chowdrisaheb used to say something in the village, someone would dictate it to him first. Only Aqeeda's father would come forward , This story is not only of two lovers but of a society whose silence can also become the reason of destruction for someone's love. It is because love is a pond whose desire is the only way and no foot is the reason for this, only one reason is that which is cruelty. To make the soul away from him. Saying it will go away soon. This secret can be told by both those whose Love has just begun. So let's see what happens next. They say that even love is such a pressure that if it is found at the right time, a person's life can be saved and if it is not found on time by mistake, it can also lead to death. Someone's love is like a poison because it kills someone, and sometimes it is only.

Shayari 1

"MOHABATT BHALEHEE SIFAR HAIMERIPER ISKI INAAYATSE SAB WAQIF HAIAUR TUM JOMUJHE MITANE KIKOSISH KAR RAHEHOUSKI KHASHISHBHI KAHI NAKAHIISHI KI KHAWISHHAI..........KUCH NAAYAABKARNE KI TALABHAIPER AFSSOS KIBAAT TOH YEHHAI KIMERI TALABHEE ABHI SIFARHAI..........."

Reality Vs Virtuality

They say no, if you want something, then you should not know that you have a pond, it is you on its destination, I mean if you have a say about something, then it will never be found by revealing ,dont do it Because the writing has already become a fate, it will never change where our thinking begins, who's handwriting ends Even though the love of Tabir and Aqeeda was God's handwriting, they did not even have the trouble to carry them forward, it is said that there is some handwriting which is also different from

God's handwriting. Like victory , his feet were not in his feet for a long time. Means Chaudhary saheb and Khan saheb who were his fathers even though he tried to join them. He thought of his shakti karan's feet, was it acceptable to everyone, was it acceptable to both of them, in which their love had stepped into the wonderful life, did they accept it. His love started with which a little poet, a little sweet, and a lot of all also said to each other. It happens that they do not know that they had come so close that they could not marry without each other. The needless feet were not like this, it was completely different from Vote, she liked to make friends, she neither lived alone like Tabeer nor like him at all times, I should say in straight words in her thinking, so this love was on the first side, my feet are nothing ahead of me Know that you will have to see for yourself that what would happen next, it was not even a matter that Aqeeda did not do hypnosis. She didn't think about him, she used to think of him as a friend only at that time, that friend who used to go to the society without saying anything to him, that friend who could fight with anyone for her, that friend who had his own life in school. Leave teaching and try to read it, and when someone asked the teacher something and he did not tell the husband, even if he himself had to bear one thing, he said one thing right, then I laughed at the handwriting of the divine God that what is this love which is being shared by each other. I don't know what it is for each other, didn't it hurt both of them? Its one sided love and one sided love is just like God's destiny which is not in everyone's part, the prisoner sees what happens, even if the age in which Tabeer was in, no one will be able to say the words of love even in my opinion. if loves is true, don't say why it is one sided and don't see anyone's words. She gets shocked. Tabir who used to think for aqeeda, probably did not hate aqeeda at the time and whatever he did for her, he never even thought about him, but still Tabir Kasab liked what he liked. May it be sweet custard, even if it is jalebi, maybe time will stop me because of the love pattern I am going to talk about. I love her dear-intes I say that when I am happy, I want to be with her say that I want to be the companion of every sorrow and happiness, before he says anything, I want to give her every happiness that is written by me. I can't express my love for her, I don't know what is the feeling that can never go away from her when I grow up, neither will I share how much I love her. Whatever these things were, he wrote in his own diary. It was because he never asked you to reveal his words in front of her , he wanted to go ahead when he is older. If he goes to his surgery, the handwriting that is in his bar will give him strength. And the love he has made with her, he will finally reveal it to her. Whatever I live in, we give up everything for them and go to a world where there is only and its friends and nothing else. you feel for someone. Not till then. and kills the flame of someone we love, after that some I don't even have to take anything from anyone because the time we get in love is the one where no one has it. The love which was one sided, now it was probably going to end soon because of the arrival of someone else for Tabeer. Don't know the name of the male witness yet see for yourself what happens next.

Shayari 1
"AJEEB NADAAMATMILI HAI TUJHECAHH KE (2)KYUNKI AAB NATOH VO NAFSHAI MERE PASSNA HEE VO WAJAHJISKE RABT SEHAMARE MEHFILHAR KOIWAQIF THA ....EK TARFA HEE SAHIPER

MOHABATT TOHTHITUJHE CAHNE KATUJHE HASIL
KARNE KAEK ZARIYA TOH THAPER BEI-GAIRATUSH
WAQT KIPARCHAI NEMUJHSEHVO BHI CHEENLIYA
........KI ITTIFAAQ SEFURQAT MILI HAIHAMEISME KOI
KHUDAKI LIKHAWAT NAHI THI (2)AUR TUM KOSISH
KAR LOHAME MITANE KIPER USSE PEHLEYEH WAQIF
KARDU (2)
KI KOI ZARIYANAHI HAI HAMARIMOHABATT
KOMITANE KI ...."

CHAPTER FOUR

The Path Of Ending

Enter Caption

1936 Today Aqeeda and Tabir are 16 years old and the love of childhood was love for Tabeer, now that love has increased a bit more than Aqeeda, whose love he has not revealed to anyone for 15 years, now that time has come and that age too. Tabir was always afraid of the same thing that if Aqeeda did not accept his love, then what would happen to him and with the help of which you had hidden all the secrets inside him, if he revealed that secret in front of Aqeed, then what would happen if he understood his condition. - Will he go through a lot of pain, will that time disappear. Seeing the timeless time he has spent his days by looking at his friends, will they end now. What is going to happen in the life of Aqeeda. In a village where it was a wish of the people that whosoever prays in front of him by shedding his blood in the river, it will be fulfilled if it is really true then undefined All the time they must be thinking that where did their love come from undefined they say that they are not incomplete. Story and incomplete love suppose always cause a dilemma, so better too know him completely. The day before Tabeer was going to tell my heart sayings Aqeeda, he also went to the bank of the river that his love was accepted and his love For that he had shed blood as well, because those peoples understand these things was foot truth, no one knows till date. Seeing that she was coming from, he also followed her. When he reached the outer, he saw that she had jumped into the river to commit suicide. He was never returning, but both of them knew that, even then, knowing this, Tabir went without caring for his life to save him. On the banks of the river , the path was always the same when those two litters could not even scratch them. what was then. Tabir saved Aqeeda. He put his life to Dr. Without thinking anything, without thinking anything. The love of love had made him the traveler of the path while he was alive. When you came out, what happened and what happened after that, you all should see for yourself. Tabir, What were you going to do? What is everything, why give yourself a path says undefined Tabeer, Aqeeda If you have ever considered me as your true friend, then look in our eyes and say what is the reason because of which you have to take such a big step Para .Aqeeda and tabeer undefined

You have to hear that our reason for birth is new, that why we have taken such a step.. Listen, you are the reason because of which I have taken education. What do you have to say and what are you going to say? What is the reason for which I am second, which crime I have committed... I have only asked you a true friend, there is no existence of love between us, neither today nor will I fall in love with anyone else whose fate is not there, I am going to tell my father, I have seen you that now elders You are going near the river at a high speed. (The sacrifice that is made in love can only be done by the society who has had true love for someone, but this day Aqeeda did not try to understand what the word she is saying in front of the Taber would have on her. only her shadow banker used to live with him all the time in search of that, he must have expressed all his pain . I don't know if you will be able to pin your love to him.) This pain was only and only to Tabeer that his father and Aqeeda's father had fixed their marriage in childhood, but he never allowed it to be revealed that they were born to be the reason for each other's existence, on the day when Aqeeda was born to Tabeer. When she went home, she heard Chaudhary sir and you father talking that we should ask for those dons soon because now the age is right that they should understand each other and our friendship should also turn into kinship. tabir, who was about to give, saw her and he also started running after her, due to which he thought of committing suicide. There is also a mystery that he is the witness after all? Who changed the handwriting of Tabeer's love? the search is not complete till date.

Shayari 1

"NA HEE KOI WAJOOD TERANA HEE KOI KASHISH
HUNPER AFSOOSTERI MOHABATT HEE VO
WAJAHHAI.............................JISKE WAJAH SE AAJ BHI
TERAMUSHAFIR HUN..........KI DARD KI TANHAIYE
HAIAUR KOI WAJAH NAHI HAIKHAMOSHI MERE
MANNKE AANDAR HAIAUR KOI WAJAH NAHI
HAIMEIN ISH HADD TAK TUTTCHUKA HUNKI KHUD
KO PECHAAN NA PA RAHA HAIPHIR BHIAUR KOI
WAJAH NAHI HAI ....DO PAHIYO KI TARAHHAM BHI
EK DUSRE KESAATHI HAITU SATH RAHE CAHE
NARAHEHAM TERE LIYE PHIR BHI EKBEI- SAKHI HAI
.........."

Change Of Life

It is said that love is the means by which we can win the world because its taste is a passion, we would go to great extent to say a desire which we have never done, love has a big hand in the making of the world because if we think of science If the world is made, love is the means, because of which it is still maintained or its strength, which is still strong, it probably does not last. The way of saying it seems completely wrong, because the pond which lives in one-way love, maybe does not live anywhere in the world, well they move ahead and know who is that witness, due to which Tabir's love remained incomplete. Salim who is Harpan Maula Sahib There was a son of the singer who was a singer by profession, nothing is known about him, he was a person who knew more by the name of Salim than the singer. Aqeeda liked him so much? Feet this word is totally wrong because he is not There was no good witness, nor did she have any say in the name of a good bane, who has achieved fate on deceit, then for love, one way arrows go to get a pond. Everyone had the same dream about her that somehow enough would become my wife and nothing else. If the enmity had arisen, there would have been some cure for her, because it is such a flame that always gives a sigh of relief to share . He was true in the world, he has found only and only way, nothing else in luck. And whose love is a deception, a means to make his pond just a wish, nothing else remains for him. Salim is such a witnes that someone love didn't make any difference because he never wanted any one girl, because love was the game in which he wanted to get fat all the time and this was also the reason for his ruin. Well let's see Salim was a public He believed that there was no one in his village to have a beautiful girl and he used to realize that He also became his wife and it happened also means that you made him fall in love with her. In return, he only gets deceit after going ahead and believing that Salim loves Salim more than himself. So he himself does not know how much he is in love with her. Salim does not feel anything like this about him, nor did he care about him Going ahead, he had achieved what he used to say and in the end, aqeeda also became a victim of his love, after that many changes had come in Aqeeda, such as he took such a Hijra from Tabir, which no one had any desire, he would meet him every day. In the same month, she used to meet him a couple of times, time changed, love increased even more. For me and for Tabir's belief. They say that when someone stays with you, you don't have any kind of foot. Which is not good for a long time, Salim, you had played games with many such girls in the village, love, I mean, Salim lived in the village next to the village where Aqeeda and Tabir lived and they also met with the words of Tabir. What did he know that in the end he would be left with an arrow? When he looked at Salim's face, he could not erase the tradition of enough happiness, because even though Aqeeda was not in love with him, the day was to Tabir, Aqeeda was going to commit suicide and the lucky Tabeer asked her that you were in love with someone else. Then what did he say. Tabir: Do you also love someone???Tabir, speak Aqeeda I am from Salim I am in love and I can't live without it, if God did not accept our relationship, then he only gave us the way. Aqeeda undefined Excuse me for being rude, I love you and I tell you to agree to it. Hadd beautiful too, then they talk about both of them and she went to her house and she explained to her father and Aqeeda's father also that if both of us get together today, I will fall in the eyes of Aqeeda We don't want love to die, I only say that the one who is in love with the one who is in love with his life is not the reason for his happiness, nor have I ever been in love with faith, so in some way I should make them a part of my existence. When I will never be able to love them Chaudhary sahib already knew that tabir lie was speaking because at the time when both of them were doing great work , what they didn't say at that time is also a question and how tabir knew salim and How did he meet Tabeer and will Zakar aqeeda come to know about Salim's truth in the future, this story will only be one-sided love of Tabeer, will Tabeer ever go ahead and tell his heart, will he be together, I will definitely tell a secret. Next, the story of society's big hand and partition is also the story , foot intestine will be in 1947's handwriting and there is one thing that going forward Salim's death will also happen, how is the society's hand in this because it is Tabir's. He used to be so infatuated with faith that there was no such evidence that could make him so infatuated with him. Can do because there are many such enmities in this part which are still there. Indo-Pak's love story is the foot forward mirror will be made for those who have made our society ....

Shayari 1

"KHUDA KI LIKHAWAT HUNMEINKISHI KI CAHAT HUNMEIN (2)TALAB TOH HARRKISHI KO HAI MERIPER AFSOOSHAR KISHI KI SIYAASAT]NAHI HUN MEIN .....HAMDAM NAHI THA TERAPHIR BHI SATH NIBHANEKI KOSHISH KI THIMOHABATT NAHI THITUJHE MUJHSEHPHIR BHI APNI LIKHAWAT TUHE DII THIAUR HA ITTIFAAQSE HEE SAHIPER USH KHUDANE MERI TAQDEER KIBANABAT TERE SATH HEEKI THI ...MERI FIKR KAZARIYA HAI TUMERI TALAB KIPECHAAN BHI (2)AUR JISH BE-SHUMAARFAROGH KI MUJHE TISHNAGIHAIUSKI

IKALAUTEE HAQADARRBHI ..."

The Waiting Period

When life gives a means, it should be seen on the right foot only once, I don't know if the next time you don't get that chance, when you have to go far away from your pond, your existence is not yours, nor do you have any regret, but alas, your love is the reason due to which Since even today I am your friend, time always seems to be due to love, because the time to change it is never in our favor, no matter how many ponds there are.......

www.ingramcontent.com/pod-product-compliance
Lightning Source LLC
Chambersburg PA
CBHW020657160726
47991CB00003B/1223